Ross Burach

scholastic press • new york

BLADDER
BUSTER
BEVERAGE CO.
NEWS
Stuff

Thanks for calling Truck Full of Ducks . . .

We'll be right there!

munch
munch
munch

OH NO! The directions!

Don’t worry, ducks.
We’ll find the customer!

Did you call for a truck full of ducks?
BLADDER BUSTER BEVERAGE Co.
TRUCK full of DUCKS
est. 1980

No, not me. I called for a mail truck.
25¢
CONTENTS:
1 Brother
Please mail
very FAR
AWAY
MAIL
MAIL

Did you call for a truck full of ducks?
D-D-D-DUCK truck?
N-N-Not me, buddy.
I called for a
D-D-D-DUMP truck.

UNDER
Construction
Humpty
Dumpty
Had A Great HAUL!
•DUMP TRUCK SERVICE•

Did you call for a truck full of ducks?
TRUCK full of DUCKS
est. 1980
Surf Shark

No, dude, not us. We called for an ice cream truck!

Who called for a truck full of ducks?

Sadie's
ICE CREAM
SANDWICHES
DELICIOUS!

Did you call for a truck full of ducks?

Arrr! It wasn't me, matey. I called for a truck full of crackers . . . not quackers!

Did you call for a truck full of ducks?

Sorry, Earthling.
I called for a tow truck.

Thirty thousand light-years away, huh? This is gonna cost ya.
TONY'S
TONY'S
TOWING
We'll TOW ANYWHERE!
I BRAKE FOR Comets & Cupcakes
KEEP BACK: I NEED MY SPACE

WHO CALLED FOR A TRUCK FULL OF DUCKS??

YOU'RE in LUCK!
LAST POTTY
For Miles

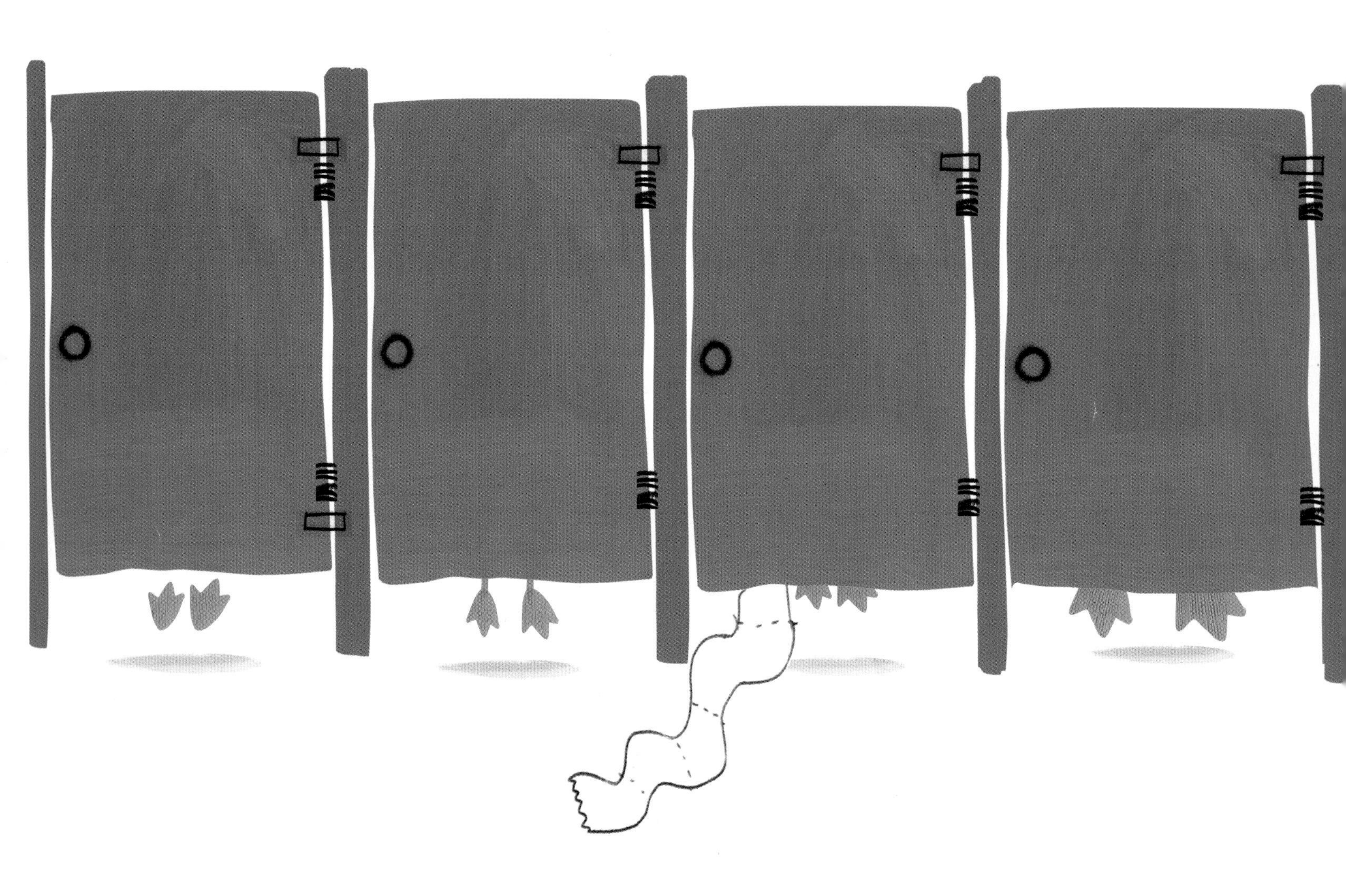

HURRY UP, ducks!

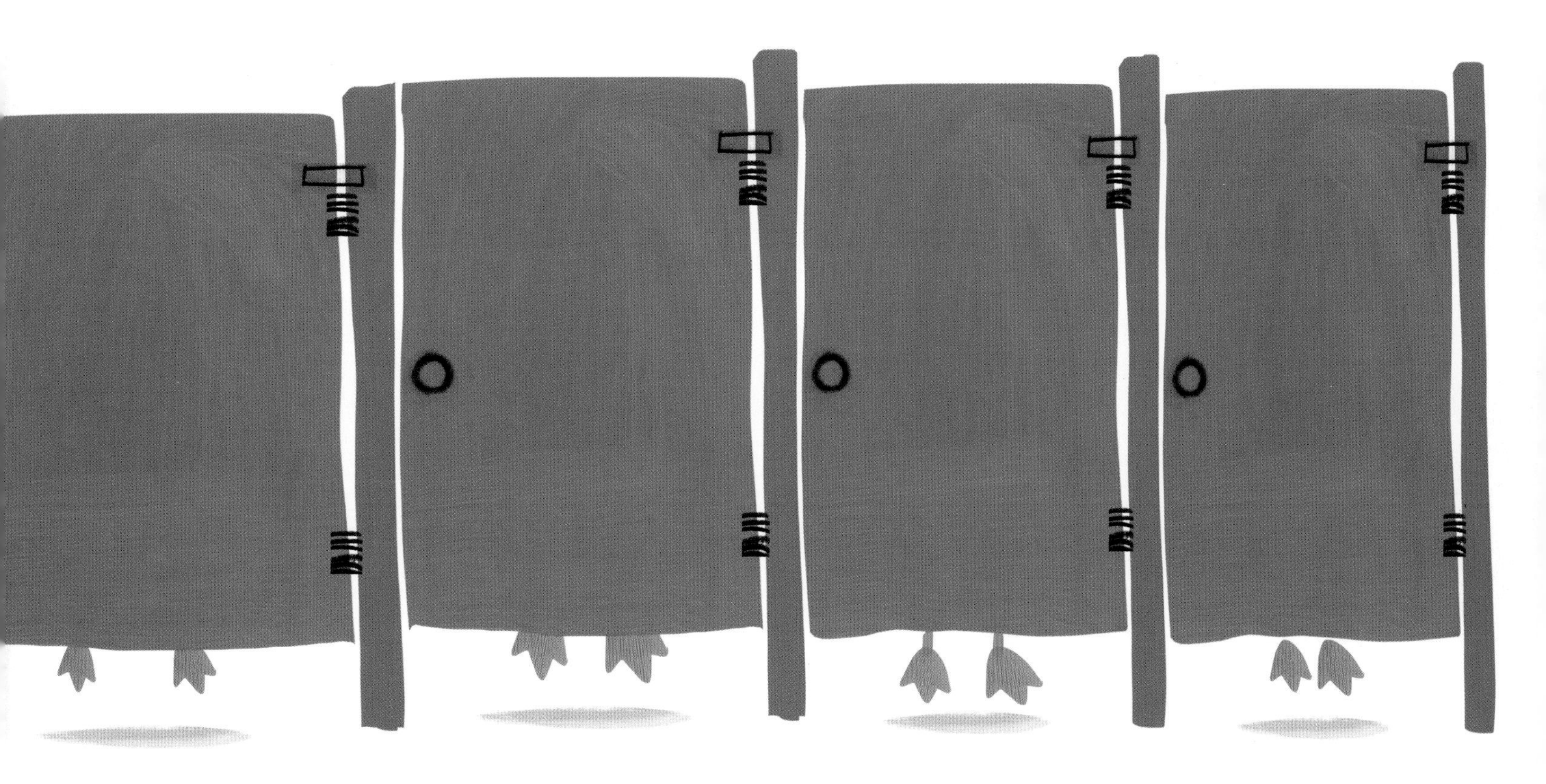

Back in the truck! The clock is ticking!

Did YOU call for a truck full of ducks?

AHHHH! NO! NO MORE DUCKS!

I called for a duck REMOVAL truck!

DID ANYONE CALL FOR A TRUCK FULL OF DUCKS?!
TRUCK full of DUCKS
est. 1980

Did you say,
“truck full of ducks”?
That was me.
DEEP
DARK
WOODS

TRUCK
full of
DUCKS
est. 1980

Over here . . .

Okay, ducks. Out of the truck!
See, I told you not to worry.

Perfect timing.
MY DINNER . . .
1
WILL
I leave my Lake house to my mom.

. . . is over!

Time for my bath!

Bath time gig, Stan?
VAN FULL of TOUCANS
VAN FULL of TOUCANS
When You Need TOUCANS... Who Can? We Can!

You know it, Frank!

TRUCK full of DUCKS

est. 1980

Thanks for calling Truck Full of Ducks . . .
We'll be right there!

To Tracy, Marijka, and Kait — one quacky crew! — R.B.

 Published by Scholastic Press, an imprint of Scholastic Inc., *Publishers since 1920.* SCHOLASTIC, SCHOLASTIC PRESS, and associated logos are trademarks and/or registered trademarks of Scholastic Inc. · The publisher does not have any control over and does not assume any responsibility for author or third-party websites or their content. · Library of Congress Cataloging-in-Publication Data available · ISBN 978-1-338-12936-6 · 10 9 8 7 6 5 4 3 2 1 18 19 20 21 22 · Printed in China 38 · First edition, April 2018 · The drawings were created with pencil, crayon, acrylic paint, and digital coloring. · The text type was set in Loyola Pro Bold and Loyola Pro. · The display type was set in Chaloops Bold. · The book was printed on 128 gsm Golden Sun Matte and bound at RR Donnelley Asia. · Production was overseen by Angie Chen. · Manufacturing was supervised by Shannon Rice. · The book was art directed by Marijka Kostiw, designed by Ross Burach and Marijka Kostiw, and edited by Tracy Mack.